FAIRY TALE DINNERS
A COOKBOOK FOR
YOUNG READERS AND EATERS

Fairy Tales retold by

Jane Yolen

Recipes by

Heidi E.Y. Stemple

Illustrations by

Philippe Béha

an imprint of
WINDMILL BOOKS™
New York

For my daughter, for meals cooked, jokes shared, and love always
—JY

*For Jen and the thousands of dinners we cooked together, for Nina whose name should
be on this book for all the help she gave me, and for all my taste testers especially my
daughters—Maddison and Glendon*
—HEYS

For my daughters Sara and Fanny
—PB

The recipes in this book are intended to be prepared with an adult's help.

Published in 2010 by Windmill Books, LLC
303 Park Avenue South, Suite # 1280, New York, NY 10010-3657

Adaptations to school & library edition © 2010 Windmill Books
Adapted from *Fairy Tale Feasts: A Literary Cookbook for Young Readers and Eaters.*
Published by arrangement with Crocodile Books, an imprint of Interlink Publishing Group, Inc.

Text copyright © 2006 Jane Yolen and Heidi E. Y. Stemple
Illustrations copyright © 2006 Philippe Béha

Publisher Cataloging Data

Yolen, Jane
       Fairy tale dinners : a cookbook for young readers and eaters – School & library ed. / fairy tales retold by Jane Yolen ;
recipes by Heidi E. Y. Stemple ; illustrations by Philippe Béha.
         p. cm. – (Fairy tale cookbooks)
       Contents: Hodja borrows a pot–The three lemons–The great turnip–Jack and the beanstalk.
       Summary: This book includes retellings of four fairy tales paired with dinner
recipes connected to each story.
       ISBN 978-1-60754-580-4 (lib.) – ISBN 978-1-60754-582-8 (pbk.)
ISBN 978-1-60754-581-1 (6-pack)
       1. Cookery–Juvenile literature   2. Dinners and dining–Juvenile literature   3. Fairy tales   [1. Cookery
2. Dinners and dining   3. Fairy tales]   I. Stemple, Heidi E. Y.   II. Béha, Philippe   III. Title   IV. Series
       641.5/123–dc22

Manufactured in the United States of America.

TABLE OF CONTENTS

HODJA BORROWS A POT

One day, one fine day, Hodja decided to make kebabs for his family, but he didn't have the right pot for the rice. So off he went to his cousin's to borrow a big copper pot.

"Bring it back first thing in the morning," said his cousin, who did not trust Hodja at all. He was *such* a fool.

But first thing in the morning, Hodja was back with the big pot and there was a little pot inside of it.

"What's this? What's this?" asked the cousin.

Hodja grinned and struck his forehead with the flat of his hand. "Indeed, I am such a fool. I have forgotten to congratulate you. Your big pot has given birth to a little pot. Allah's blessings."

His cousin laughed, loud and long. What a fool Hodja was! "Thank you for your congratulations and may Allah bless you, too." Then his cousin took both pots into her kitchen.

• • •

This Turkish tale is typical of many of the short, pithy jest stories featuring the wise fool known as Hodja or Nasr-ed-Din Hodja. (The word "hodja" in old Turkey simply meant a Moslem scholar and teacher.) He can also be found in stories throughout the Middle East, where he is also called Jawha or Goha.

Some scholars believe there was an actual man named Hodja about whom these stories were told. In 1960 the Turkish government published an official collection of Nasr-ed-Din Hodja stories, and there is a government sanctioned tombstone for him at Akeshehiz, with the date 1284.

Not a week later, Hodja came back to borrow the big pot once again and, of course, hoping for another increase, the cousin loaned it to him.

"Bring it back first thing in the morning," she reminded him.

But Hodja did not bring the pot back that morning, nor the next, nor the next. A week went by, then two, and finally, exasperated, Hodja's cousin knocked on his door.

When Hodja answered, she shook her finger in his face. "Where is my pot? It is my best pot and I have friends coming to visit."

Hodja tore at his hair. "Alas," he cried, "I feared to tell you. It is so sad. The very night I borrowed your poor cauldron—Allah's ways are not to be questioned—the pot died!"

"Died?" cried the cousin. "How can you say such a thing? A pot cannot die."

Hodja smiled sweetly. "If a pot can give birth," he said, "then surely it can die."

Not such a fool after all, was Nasr-ed-Din Hodja. ⭐

Hodja's Kebabs

If you want rice, don't lend your cousin your pot. (Serves a family)

Yogurt Marinade

EQUIPMENT:

- medium bowl

- garlic press

- spoon

INGREDIENTS:

- 1 cup plain yogurt (230 ml)

- 1 clove of garlic, pressed

- ½ tsp. salt

- ¼ tsp. pepper

- ¼ tsp. cumin

Lemon Marinade

EQUIPMENT:

*Same as
Yogurt Marinade*

INGREDIENTS:

- Juice from 1–2 lemons
  (approximately ½ cup
  or 115 ml)

- ½ cup olive oil (115 ml)

- 2 cloves of garlic, pressed

- 1 tsp. salt

- ¼ tsp. pepper

*Facts about kebab:
1. A kebab is a
dish of meat, and
sometimes vegetables,
that are roasted on
skewers.
2. The word
"kebab" comes from
the Arabic* kabb,
*which means cooked
meat in small pieces,
or possibly from
the Aramaic* kabb
*meaning burning or
charring.
3. Shish-kebab
consists of cubes of
meat like lamb, beef,
or chicken grilled
on skewers. Adana
kebab is spicy meat
patties on skewers,
doner kebab is the
Greek gyro, tandir
kebab is pit-roasted
lamb.*

4. Kebab is essentially a Turkish dish that goes back to the time when the Turks were nomads grilling meat over campfires. The kebab spread through the Arab and Greek worlds.

5. In Turkey, an inexpensive kebab restaurant is called a kebabci.

DIRECTIONS:

1. Choose a marinade.

2. Mix all ingredients in a bowl.

Meat

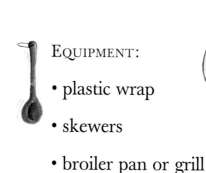

EQUIPMENT:

- plastic wrap
- skewers
- broiler pan or grill

INGREDIENTS:

- chicken, lamb, beef, or shrimp
- vegetables such as peppers, onions, mushrooms, and tomatoes (optional)

DIRECTIONS:

1. Choose chicken, lamb, beef, or shrimp.

2. Clean and cut meat into cubes; devein and peel shrimp.

3. Add to marinade of choice, cover with plastic wrap, and refrigerate for at least 1 hour.

4. Put meat on skewer, alternating with vegetables if you wish.

5. Cook on the grill or approximately 4 inches under the broiler on broiler pan (to catch juices away from kebabs) for 4–6 minutes

per side for meat or until cooked to desired doneness. Chicken should be cooked entirely with no pink left in the middle. Check by cutting open a middle piece. Beef or lamb can be left pink in the middle and is a personal choice by the eater. For shrimp, cook 1½–2 minutes or until pinkish in color.

Serve with rice or with flat bread and vegetables.

THE THREE LEMONS

Once there was a king with only one son. For many years the prince refused to marry. But one day, when the prince was cutting apart a cream tart, he accidentally sliced his finger. A single drop of his blood fell into the cream and he was suddenly seized with the desire to find a wife who was as white as cream and red as blood.

The king was so pleased that his son was finally willing to marry, he gave his blessing. "Go, my boy. Find your heart's desire."

So off rode the prince, through farmyards and villages, along coastlines and up into the high mountains, looking for such a girl.

At last he came upon an old woman sitting under a tree, with a basket of fruit and cakes by her side. Being a polite young man, the prince inquired if she were just resting or needed help.

"Neither, dear boy, I have been waiting for you," she said. "Tell me why you wander so far from home."

So he told her his story, and when he was done, she presented him with three lemons. "As you were kind to me, I shall help you get your heart's desire. Go home, and along your way stop at the

This Italian story can be found all over Europe.

A similar Norwegian tale, with the same name, stars three brothers instead of a single prince, and a hag, plus a swarm of trolls instead of the one old lady. The girls in the lemons are not fairies, but princesses. And the serving girl is a cook. But the story itself remains the same.

very first well you see. There cut one of these lemons in half. A fairy will come out of it and ask for water. You must get it at once or she will disappear. The same with the second lemon, and the third. Do not let the third fairy disappear for she will be the wife of your heart."

The prince was delighted, and he bid the old wise woman farewell, then started for home.

• • •

It was not long before he came to a well that was in a lovely copse of trees. There he dismounted and took out the first of the three lemons. With his knife, he sliced through the lemon and—in a flash—a beautiful girl appeared, as white as cream and with lips as red as strawberries.

"I need a drink of water!" she cried.

The prince was so dazzled by her that he was slow to do as she asked and, in an instant, she was gone.

So he reached into his saddlebag and took out the second lemon, then cut it open. A second fairy, more beautiful than the first, came out and demanded a drink. But once again the prince was slow and she, too, disappeared.

The prince knew that he dared not lose the third fairy, so this time he drew the water up from the well first. Then he cut open the final lemon, and when the third fairy appeared, he was ready and handed her a ladle-full of water.

When she had drunk her fill, the fairy turned to the prince and said, "Now, my prince, we shall be wed."

He could not believe his happiness. "Let me go home and return with an escort worthy of you, to lead you in splendor to my father's palace."

The fairy agreed and as soon as the prince was out of sight, she climbed into the fork of a tree overlooking the well so that she could watch all that happened but could not, herself, be seen.

No sooner had she climbed the tree than a hideous girl, the daughter of a mean mother and a meaner father, arrived at the well with a jar that needed filling. The girl was so ugly, her nose and chin threatened to meet in the middle and she had hardly three hairs on the top of her head.

As she leaned over the well, she saw reflected in it the face of the fairy in the tree. Now the hideous girl had never seen herself in any mirror, for her parents refused to have them in the house, and she thought the face was her own. Aloud she said, "Why Caramella, you are beautiful and should not be made to work a day longer."

Then she broke her mother's jar and capered around it. She looked so peculiar doing that, the fairy in the tree began to laugh.

Caramella glanced up and saw the fairy. In that instance, she realized the face she had seen in the well had been this beautiful creature's, not her own. Suddenly fearing she would be beaten by

Related to the "Forgotten Fiancee" stories this tale has relatives in the folk music world as well. The song "The Nut Brown Maiden" is the story of a prince being duped into marrying the wrong girl.

In every instance of the tale, the deception is found out, the bad girl punished, and the princess/fairy finally returned to her proper position.

13

her mother for breaking the jar, Caramella said slyly: "Why are you in the tree, pretty maiden?"

The fairy saw no reason not to tell her. In that instant, Caramella decided on a wicked plan. "Let me comb your hair so that when the prince returns, you will be more beautiful than before."

The fairy agreed and climbed down. But while Caramella combed her hair, she struck the fairy with a pointed shard of the jar, to kill her. The moment the shard touched the fairy's head she cried out, "Dove!" and turned into a snow-white bird. Then she flew away over the trees and out of sight.

• • •

Soon after, the prince returned with his escort. Imagine his surprise when he was greeted by the hideous Caramella who said, "Oh, my prince, I am indeed the fairy from the third lemon, but I have been enchanted by a wizard into this awful form."

The prince felt that he was to blame, having left his beloved behind, so he took the ugly girl home, dressed in the splendid bridal clothes he had brought with him.

His father the king and his mother the queen did not dare say a word against Caramella for she was their son's choice of a bride.

A great wedding was planned, and every king and queen from far and wide was invited.

Now, as the cook was preparing the wedding feast, a snow-white dove with a red beak flew into the window and cried:

Alas, the prince and the false bride are wed,
While lives the true bride, both white and red.

The cook ran and told the king and queen who told the prince. The prince came into the kitchen and caught the white bird. As soon as he touched it, the bird turned back into the fairy, who told him how the hideous Caramella had tried to murder her.

"Wait here," he said, "behind the curtain." Then he returned to the wedding feast and addressed his guests. "What," he asked, "should be done to someone who tries to kill my beloved bride?"

They shouted out horrible punishments. "Such a one should be stoned!" And "Put in a barrel filled with vipers!" But Caramella said, "Burn her to death and scatter the ashes to the four winds."

The prince nodded. "You have pronounced your own death, wicked girl," he said. And it was done.

Then the prince married his real bride, whom he found in a lemon, and they lived happily ever after. ⭐

Lemon Chicken

No fairies in this lemon dish, but no sourpuss either. (Makes 3–4 servings)

Facts about lemons:
1. The lemon is the berry of its tree.
2. The lemon fruit is actually green and not particularly sour. For lemons to become yellow and tart, the tree must grow where temperatures dip below 50 degrees F (10 degrees C) but always remain above freezing.
3. A lemon has 18 calories, and no fat or cholesterol, as well as 35 percent of the daily recommendation of Vitamin C.

EQUIPMENT:

- measuring spoons
- small bowl
- spoon
- cutting board
- sharp knife
- measuring cup (heat proof)
- large skillet or electric skillet with a top
- spatula

INGREDIENTS:

- 4 tbsp. butter (half stick) (60 g)
- 3 boneless, skinless chicken split breasts
- 2 tbsp. flour
- 1 tsp. tarragon
- 1 cube chicken bouillon dissolved in ¾ cup hot water (175 ml) (or ¾ cup stock)
- 1 lemon

DIRECTIONS:

1. Rinse the chicken in cool water.

2. Cut the chicken lengthwise into 1-inch (2.5 cm) strips.

3. Mix the flour and tarragon in the small bowl. Set aside.

4. Slice the lemon into thin slices. Discard the ends. Set aside.

5. Melt butter in the skillet at medium-high heat.

6. Place chicken into skillet and, while cooking, sprinkle a small spoonful of the flour/tarragon mixture on top of the chicken.

7. Mix with spatula constantly to coat and cook it evenly.

8. Sprinkle more flour/tarragon and repeat until all is in the pan and the chicken is cooked through.

9. Reduce heat to low.

10. Pour water/bouillon mixture over the chicken.

11. Top with lemons and cover. Let simmer for a minute.

12. Stir once and cover again, cooking for another minute or two.

13. Pour or spoon the entire dish onto a serving platter, slowly so as not to splash the juice and burn yourself.

SERVING SUGGESTIONS:

Try serving lemon chicken with Caesar salad, rice, and garlic bread.

4. Scholars believe that the lemon originated in China, Persia, or the Indus Valley. By the second century, lemons were exported from Libya to Rome. We know this because a mosaic in the ruins of the city of Pompeii shows a lemon.

5. The ladies of Louis XIV's court in France used lemons to redden their lips.

6. The rind of the lemon is called the zest. It holds tiny sacs of lemon oil, and can be used in recipes.

THE GREAT TURNIP

Once in old Russia, Grandfather planted a turnip. The turnip grew and grew and grew some more. It grew until it was huge, the size of a pot.

Grandfather came out of the house, puffing on his pipe. He tried to pull the turnip out. He pulled and pulled but the great turnip would not come out of the ground.

"Grandmother," he called, "help me pull this great turnip out of the ground for it is huge, the size of a pot."

So Grandmother came out of the house, a babushka on her head. She put her arms around Grandfather's waist and they pulled and they pulled but the great turnip would not come out of the ground.

Grandmother called to her daughter, "Masha, come and help us pull this great turnip out of the ground for it is huge, the size of a pot."

So Masha came out of the house, wiping her hands on her apron. She put her arms around Grandmother's shoulders and Grandmother had her arms around Grandfather's waist, and they pulled and they pulled but the great turnip would not come out of the ground.

Masha called to her dog, "Sasha, come out here and help us pull this great turnip out of the ground for it is huge, the size of a pot."

Then out came the dog, shaking his ears. He grabbed the ties on Masha's apron and Masha put her arms around Grandmother's shoulders and Grandmother had her arms around Grandfather's waist, and they pulled and they pulled but the great turnip would not come out of the ground.

Sasha barked to the cat, "Mischa, come out here and help us pull this great turnip out of the ground for it is huge, the size of a pot."

Then out came the cat, preening his whiskers. He grabbed the dog's tail and the dog grabbed the ties on Masha's apron and Masha put her arms around Grandmother's shoulders and Grandmother had her arms around Grandfather's waist, and they pulled and they pulled but the great turnip would not come out of the ground.

Mischa meowed to the mouse, "Kasha, come out here and help us pull this great turnip out of the ground for it is huge, the size of a pot."

Out came the mouse, eating a piece of cheese, and she pulled on the cat's tail, and the cat grabbed the dog's tail and the dog grabbed the ties on Masha's apron and Masha put her arms around Grandmother's shoulders and Grandmother had her arms around Grandfather's waist, and they pulled and they pulled.

Kasha pulled Mischa, Mischa pulled Sasha, Sasha pulled Masha, Masha pulled Grandmother, Grandmother pulled Grandfather and the huge turnip . . . came out of the ground. Then they all went inside the house and had turnip for dinner. ⭐

This is a familiar cumulative tale, the kind of story especially popular with the youngest story lovers. It is often told in kindergartens, with all the children joining in. Almost like a game, cumulative tales invite the listener to recite along with them. Think of "This is House that Jack Built" and "The Gingerbread Man." They are cumulative stories as well.

Mashed Turnips

You can work up quite an appetite with all that pulling. (Serves a family)

EQUIPMENT:

- cutting board
- sharp knife
- medium-sized pan
- colander
- measuring cup
- bowl
- potato masher or electric mixer

INGREDIENTS:

- 1 large or 4 small turnips
- ⅛ cup milk (30 ml)
- stick of butter (115 g) (though you can use less)
- ½ tsp. salt
- ⅛ tsp. pepper
- extra salt for boiling water

DIRECTIONS:

1. Peel and cut turnip(s) into 1-inch (2.5 cm) by 3-inch (7 cm) strips.

2. Put the turnip pieces in a pan and cover with water. Add a dash of salt and bring to a boil; then reduce heat to medium high.

3. Boil for approximately 30 minutes, until the turnips are tender (can be checked with a fork).

4. Put the colander in the sink, then pour out the turnips and water into it. Rinse with hot tap water.

5. In the bowl, mash the turnips, butter, milk, salt, and pepper by hand with the potato masher or with the electric mixer.

6. When done, it will still be lumpy.

IF YOU DON'T HAVE TURNIPS, TRY THESE OTHER MASHED TUBERS:

Mashed Potatoes

Follow the same directions with 5 or 6 large potatoes. Use only half a stick of butter and potatoes may need more milk, so start with the ⅛ cup (30 ml) and add a little more at a time as needed. When done, they will be smooth.

Mashed Yams or Butternut Squash:

Follow the same directions with 4 large yams or 1 or 2 butternut squash. You will need to remove the seed and stringy middle from the squash. Use only half a stick of butter and no milk. Add 1–2 tablespoons of brown sugar. 🍅

JACK AND THE BEANSTALK

Long ago, a poor woman lived in a remote village. Her husband had been killed years earlier and all his money taken, so she and her son Jack lived in poverty in a small cottage.

Now one day even the cow stopped giving milk so there was nothing to do but sell it. So the woman called her son and said, "Jack, take Bossy to market and get the very best you can for her. Without money, we will surely starve."

So Jack took the cow and they went along and they went along until they met a strange man on the road.

"Where are you going, Jack?" asked the man, and indeed it was strange that he knew Jack's name.

"I am going to market to sell our cow," said Jack. "For without a good price for her, my mother and I shall surely starve."

"I have just the thing," said the man and he took off his hat and shook something into his hand. "Magic beans," he said showing them to Jack. "Nothing better."

So Jack gave him the cow and went home well satisfied with his trade. But when he told his mother what he had exchanged for the cow, she put her apron up over her head and wept. "Jack,

The publishing history of this particular tale begins with a tract called "Round about our Coal-Fire" printed in London in 1730. The story of "Jack Spriggins and the Enchanted Bean" is only a chapter in it.

Seventy years later, the story was published by itself as "The History of Mother Twaddle, and The Marvelous Achievements of Her Son Jack."

Jack, those beans are worthless." She took them from him and flung them out of the window. Then they both went to bed hungry.

• • •

But the beans were magic! During the night they grew and grew into a tall beanstalk. When Jack woke up, he saw the beanstalk out of his window, thick as a cow's middle and green as a fairy's coat. He jumped up and ran out to the garden. The beanstalk formed a kind of ladder that ran right up into the sky.

"If I climb up," Jack thought, "perhaps I will find my fortune there." But being a good boy, he first went back to tell his mother.

Well, she begged and pleaded for him to stay at home. "You will break my heart, and your head besides," she said.

"But Mother, if I have done wrong by selling the cow for a handful of beans, surely I will do right by finding where the magic beanstalk leads."

"Magic is not for the likes of us," she said. "It was the death of your father. He had some bits and pieces of magic, and was killed for them."

Well, it was the first Jack had ever heard of this. He thought his father had been killed by thieves. Still, ignoring his mother's pleas, he went out to the garden again and began to climb. It took hours, and of course Jack was starving, having missed dinner the night before and all the meals that day. But still he went up and up and up, until the earth below him was obscured by clouds.

And then, quite suddenly, he reached the top, where the beanstalk spread out like a path. The path turned into a road. The road into a highway. Soon Jack saw before him an enormous house.

Standing before the door of the house was the tallest woman Jack had ever seen, clearly five times his size. Why, he barely came up to her knee, and him almost a man.

"Go away, boy!" she called when she noticed him. "For my husband is a giant and he eats the flesh of humans. Why, he is off right now scouring the countryside for any meat he can find."

The idea of this giantess's husband quite terrified Jack, but he had been climbing all day without a bite to eat or a sip of water. He was tired and frantic and knew he had not the strength to turn around and go home.

"Please hide me, for just one night," he begged, "and I will be gone at first light."

Well, the good woman—for though she was a giantess, she had a fine heart—agreed. She fed him and gave him plenty to drink as well. Then she hid him in the oven. And just in time. For no sooner had Jack curled up to sleep for the night, then her husband returned, calling out,

> Fe, fi, fo, fum,
> I smell the blood of an Englishman.
> Be he alive or be he dead,
> I'll grind his bones to make my bread.

There are many Jack stories, in both British and American folklore. In them, Jack is the hero, the trickster, and sometimes the fool as well.

The famous rhyme said by the giant actually differs from story to story. Instead of

> Be he alive
> or be he dead
> I'll grind his bones
> to make my bread,

one American version ends:

> I'll grind his bones
> To eat with my
> pones.

Jack's teeth began to rattle, his knees to knock. He peeked out through a crack in the oven door.

The giantess answered, "What you smell are the humans in the dungeon, dear."

So the giant sat down at the kitchen table and said, "Bring me my hen and my harp." And as soon as his wife brought the hen and the harp, the giant picked them both up and said:

> *Lay, hen, lay,*
> *Play, harp, play,*
> *Ease me through*
> *This difficult day.*

No sooner had the giant said these words then the hen laid a golden egg and the harp began to play by itself, a tune so wonderfully soothing, that the giant fell immediately to sleep and began to snore. And beside him his wife slept, too.

Quickly, quietly, Jack opened the oven door, picked up the little hen, and stuffed it into his pocket. He grabbed up the singing harp and slung it over his shoulder. Then he found a great key on a rack and went down to the dungeon, where he freed all of the people who were destined to be the giant's supper. After that, he sneaked outside.

But no sooner was he out, then the hen began to cackle and the harp began to sing, "Master! Master!"

The giant awoke and started toward the door. Jack could hear his great feet slamming against the floor.

So Jack ran to the beanstalk. Then hand over hand, with the hen flapping about in his pocket and the harp singing out for help, he began to climb down.

The giant came fast behind him, the beanstalk shaking with his weight.

When Jack neared the bottom, he cried out, "Mother, Mother, quick fetch me Father's ax!"

She did just that and the minute Jack's feet touched the good earth, he chopped away at the beanstalk until he had chopped clean through. The beanstalk fell over and the giant hit the ground so hard, he died in an instant.

When Jack showed the hen and harp to his mother, she was not surprised. "Why, that is your father's own hen that lays golden eggs and the harp that soothes a hurting heart. I never thought to find them again, not after the giant stole what was ours."

So Jack and his mother never had to worry about money again, nor the countryside about giants. And everyone lived quite happily ever after. Except, of course, the giant. ⭐

Jack's Magic Party Beans

No humans were harmed in the making of this recipe, and still it's hearty enough for a giant. (Makes enough for a party)

EQUIPMENT:

- sharp knife
- cutting board
- frying pan
- spatula
- tongs
- paper towels on a plate
- colander (optional)
- crock-pot or large pot
- can opener
- measuring spoons
- measuring cup
- large spoon

INGREDIENTS:

- 1 package or 1 pound bacon (450 g)
- 1 pound ground beef (450 g)
- ½ onion, chopped
- 1½ tsp. dried mustard
- ¼ cup ketchup (60 ml)
- 3 tbsp. black strap molasses
- ¾ cup dark brown sugar (150 g)
- Beans: 3–8 cans of several varieties such as pork and beans, navy, white, and kidney

DIRECTIONS:

1. Cut the bacon into inch-long (2.5 cm) strips and place in the frying pan. Fry over medium heat, moving the bacon occasionally with the spatula, until completely cooked and crispy. When done, remove the bacon from the pan with tongs and place on top of a plate covered with paper towels to soak the grease out.

2. Pour off the grease from the pan when it is cooled a bit (so as not to spatter and burn yourself) and put the ground beef and the chopped onion in the frying pan to cook. Cook over medium high heat until all the beef is brown. Pour off the grease or pour everything into a colander.

3. Put the drained beef and onion mixture and the bacon into the large pot and set the heat to medium. Or, in the crock-pot, set to low for all-day cooking.

4. Open and drain the cans of beans.

5. Add the mustard, ketchup, vinegar, molasses, dark brown sugar, and the beans to the pot.

6. Cook this dish until heated through, or leave on low in the crock-pot until time to serve.

4. Broad beans and soybeans originated in Europe, but the rest were originally grown in the Americas by the native peoples. The common bean is believed to have first been cultivated in southern Mexico and Central America over 7,000 years ago.
5. The Greeks and Romans used the broad bean for voting. The white seeds meant agreement; the black seeds disagreement.
6. While beans are easy to grow, they are also easily susceptible to diseases like rusts, blights, and wilts.

For more great fiction and nonfiction, go to windmillbooks.com.